Arthur D. Innes

Verse Translations From Greek and Latin Poets

chiefly passages chosen for translation at sight

Arthur D. Innes

Verse Translations From Greek and Latin Poets
chiefly passages chosen for translation at sight

ISBN/EAN: 9783337188368

Printed in Europe, USA, Canada, Australia, Japan

Cover: Foto ©Andreas Hilbeck / pixelio.de

More available books at **www.hansebooks.com**

SEERS AND SINGERS
A Study of Five Poets

Cloth antique extra, gilt top, 5s.

———

If any other publishers have it in them to give us so pleasant a volume, the sooner they turn critics the better.—*Daily Chronicle.*

Eminently wholesome, vigorous, and suggestive. . . . —*The Academy.*

Of them all he says things one is glad to read, to applaud, and to dispute. . . .—*The Speaker.*

Much independence of judgment united to deep and luminous insight.—*St. James's Budget.*

Never were great poets and their gifts to us dealt with in a more reverential and yet discriminating fashion.—*Pall Mall Gazette.*

Clear, vivacious, unpretentious, unaffected. — *The Literary World.*

One of the best introductions to the works of Robert Browning. . . .—*The Liverpool Mercury.*

VERSE TRANSLATIONS

FROM

GREEK AND LATIN POETS

VERSE TRANSLATIONS

FROM GREEK
AND LATIN POETS

CHIEFLY OF PASSAGES CHOSEN

FOR TRANSLATION AT SIGHT

RENDERED BY

ARTHUR D. INNES

M.A., SOMETIME SCHOLAR

OF ORIEL COLLEGE

OXFORD

LONDON

A. D. INNES & CO.

BEDFORD STREET

1894

Edinburgh : T. and A. CONSTABLE, Printers to Her Majesty

PREFACE

THE verses in this volume were originally written for the most part as 'fair copies' for schoolmasters who wished to help their pupils to realise that poetry may lurk concealed behind difficulties of grammar and vocabulary. I venture to hope that, as they have been found useful for that specific purpose, they may also prove of some interest to scholars in general.

Both the text and the rendering of passages here and there are doubtful. In such cases, I have not felt bound to follow the highest

7

authority, provided that the text or rendering adopted has reasonable support.

My thanks are due for much assistance to many friends, but especially to H. C. F. Mason (Haileybury) and R. C. Gilson (Harrow).

A. D. I.

CONTENTS

9

CONTENTS

VERSE TRANSLATIONS

BATTLE-SONG

Ἄγετ', ὦ Σπάρτας εὐάνδρου
κοῦροι πατέρων πολιατᾶν,
λαιᾷ μὲν ἴτυν προβάλεσθε,
δόρυ δεξιτέρᾳ δ' εὐτόλμως·
μὴ φειδόμενοι τᾶς ζωᾶς·
οὐ γὰρ πάτριον τᾷ Σπάρτᾳ.

Sons of Sparta, mother of men,
Forward to the fight again !
With the left hand rear the shield,
With the right the war-spear wield :
Never spare your lives to-day !
That was never Sparta's way.

TYRTAEUS.

ΑΝΤΙΠΑΤΗΡ

οὐκέτι θελγομένας, Ὀρφεῦ, δρύας, οἰκέτι
πέτρας
ἄξεις, οὐ θηρῶν αὐτονόμους ἀγέ-
λας·
οὐκέτι κοιμάσεις ἀνέμων βρόμον, οὐχὶ
χάλαζαν
οὐ νιφετῶν συρμοὺς, οὐ παταγεῦσαν
ἅλα.
ὤλεο γάρ· σὲ δὲ πολλὰ κατωδύραντο
θύγατρες
Μναμοσύνας, ματὴρ δ᾽ ἔξοχα Καλ-
λιόπα.

ORPHEUS

No more, no more thy witcheries, sweet Orpheus,
    shall enthral
The oaks, the rocks, the tameless things that
    roam at will the wild ;
    No more to slumber shalt thou lull the
    moaning of the breeze,
    The hail, the sweeping snow-storms, the
    babbling of the seas ;
For thou art fallen ; and grievously for thee
    wept every child
Of Mem'ry, but Calliope thy mother more than
    all.

CL. CLAVDIANVS

FELIX qui patruis aeuum transegit
in agris,
ipsa domus puerum quem uidet,
ipsa senem ;

qui baculo nitens, in qua reptauit
arena,
unius numerat saecula longa
casae.

Illum non uario traxit fortuna
tumultu,
nec bibit ignotas mobilis hospes
aquas :

THE YEOMAN

THRICE happy, who has passed the days
  Amid the fields his fathers held,
  Whose home is still, in time of eld,
The home that knew his boyhood's ways.

To-day the staff supports his frame
  E'en where the infant crept of yore ;
  He counts the lengthening record o'er
Of that one cottage, still the same.

The 'wildering freaks of fortune's hand
  Have never dragged him up and down ;
  Nor drinks he from a stream unknown,
A houseless stranger in the land.

non freta mercator tremuit, non
    classica miles,
non rauci lites pertulit ille
    fori :

indocilis rerum, uicinae nescius
    urbis,
adspectu fruitur liberiore poli.

Frugibus alternis, non consule,
    computat annum,
auctumnum pomis, uer sibi flore
    notat.

Idem condit ager soles, idemque
    reducit,
metiturque suo rusticus orbe
    diem.

THE YEOMAN

No merchant he, for seas to scare ;
  No soldier, dreading trumpet calls ;
  Not his within the echoing walls
The clamour of debate to bear.

Small skill in things of State has he—
  He scarce has seen the town hard by ;
  In unchecked sweep of air and sky
He finds his simple pleasure free.

By changing crops the years he tells,
  Not by the names the consuls bore ;
  He marks the autumn by her store,
The spring-tide by her blossom-bells.

The fields that saw the sunset glow,
  They see the morning glory shine,
  And measure out the day's decline
By the same arching sky they know.

Ingentem meminit paruo qui ger-
  mine quercum,
aequaeuumque uidet consenu-
  isse nemus ;

proxima cui nigris Verona remo-
  tior Indis,
  Benacumque putat litora rubra
  lacum.

Sed tamen indomitae uires, fir-
  misque lacertis
  aetas robustum tertia cernit
  auum.

Erret, et extremos alter scrutetur
  Iberos ;
  plus habet hic uitae, plus habet
  ille uiae.

EPIGRAM ii.

THE YEOMAN

The spreading oak his memory knows
  Since that slim sapling whence it grew ;
  And year by year the wood he knew
That year by year beside him grows.

Verona's walls are hard at hand—
  For him, the Indies are as near ;
  For him, though close, Benacus Mere
Is distant as the Red Gulf's strand.

Yet does his vigour nowise fail,
  The brawny thews are firmly set ;
  His children's children proudly yet
Mark their old grandsire strong and hale.

So let another roving fare,
  Explore Iberia's farthest bound ;
  He has the larger range of ground,
But this of Life the richer share.

ΑΡΙΣΤΟΦΑΝΗΣ

εἴ τις ὑμῶν, ὦ θεαταί, τὴν ἐμὴν ἰδὼν
    φι´σιν
εἶτα θαυμάζει μ' ὁρᾶν μέσον διεσφηκω-
    μένον,
ἥτις ἡμῶν ἐστιν ἡ 'πίνοια τῆς ἐγκεν-
    τρίδος   •
ῥᾳδίως ἐγὼ διδάξω, κἂν ἄμουσος ᾖ τὸ
    πρίν.
ἐσμὲν ἡμεῖς οἷς πρόσεστι τοῦτο τοὐρροπύ-
    γιον
Ἀττικοὶ μόνοι δικαίως εὐγενεῖς αὐτό-
    χθονες
ἀνδρικώτατον γένος καὶ πλεῖστα τήνδε τὴν
    πόλιν

WASPS OF ATHENS

NOW if there be among you one who marked
    my shape, and so
    Fell a-wondering as my wasp-waist so slender
    he inspected,
The reason of our stings I will quickly let him
    know,
    Though until to-day his education may have
    been neglected.
For we who wear the tails you see are sprung
    of noble breed,
    Rightly claiming as the sole true-born sons
    of Attic soil ;
A race of mighty prowess, who gave succour in
    her need

ΑΡΙΣΤΟΦΑΝΗΣ

ὠφελῆσαν ἐν μάχαισιν, ἡνίκ' ἦλθ' ὁ βάρ-
βαρος,
τῷ καπνῷ τύφων ἅπασαν τὴν πόλιν καὶ
πυρπολῶν,
ἐξελεῖν ἡμῶν μενοινῶν πρὸς βίαν τ' ἀν-
θρήνια.
εὐθέως γὰρ ἐκδραμόντες ξὺν δόρι ξὺν
ἀσπίδι
ἐμαχόμεσθ' αὐτοῖσι, θυμὸν ὀξίνην πεπω-
κότες,
στὰς ἀνὴρ παρ' ἄνδρ' ὑπ' ὀργῆς τὴν
χελύνην ἐσθίων.
ὑπὸ δὲ τῶν τοξευμάτων οὐκ ἦν ἰδεῖν τὸν
οὐρανόν.
ἀλλ' ὅμως ἀπωσάμεσθα ξὺν θεοῖς πρὸς
ἑσπέραν,
γλαῦξ γὰρ ἡμῶν πρὶν μάχεσθαι τὸν στρά-
τον διέπτατο.
εἶτα δ' εἰπόμεσθα, θυννάζοντες εἰς τοὺς
θυλάκους

24

To the city, with the foremost, when the
stranger came to spoil.
He smothered with his clouds of smoke the
city, burning wide,
And most cruelly he craved to make havoc
of our nest ;
But armed with spear and shield, forth we
dashed to quell his pride,
And the rage that we had drunken was gall
in every breast.
With shoulder stanch to shoulder an angry lip
we gnawed,
While beyond their myriad arrows not a man
could see the sky ;
At fall of eve we drave them, by the succour of
the god,
For before the fight the Owl o'er our host was
hovering nigh.
We speared them through the breeches, as we
followed on our foes,

ΑΡΙΣΤΟΦΑΝΗΣ

οἱ δ' ἔφευγον τὰς γνάθους καὶ τὰς ὀφρῦς
κεντούμενοι·
ὥστε παρὰ τοῖς βαρβάροισι πανταχοῦ καὶ
νῦν ἔτι
μηδὲν Ἀττικοῦ καλεῖσθαι σφηκὸς ἀνδρι-
κώτερον.

VESPAE, 1071.

And thus goaded from our clenched jaws
and bended brows they fled ;
And through all the strangers' land to this day
the saying goes,
' There is nothing more courageous than an
Attic wasp to dread.'

ΚΛΕΑΝΘΗΣ •

Κύδιστ' ἀθανάτων, πολυώνυμε, παγκρατὲς
  αἰεί
Ζεῦ, φύσεως ἀρχηγέ, νόμου μέτα πάντα
  κυβερνῶν,
χαῖρε· σὲ γὰρ πάντεσσι θέμις θνητοῖσι
  προσαυδᾶν.
ἐκ σοῦ γὰρ γένος ἐσμὲν, ὑδῆς τίμημα
  λαχόντες
μοῦνοι ὅσα ζώει τε καὶ ἔρπει θνήτ' ἐπὶ
  γαῖαν.
τῷ σε καθυμνήσω, καὶ σὸν κράτος αἰὲν
  ἀείσω.
σοὶ δὴ πᾶς ὅδε κόσμος ἑλισσόμενος περὶ
  γαῖαν
πείθεται ᾗ κεν ἄγῃς καὶ ἑκὼν ὑπὸ σεῖο
  κρατεῖται.

THE HYMN OF CLEANTHES

FIRST of Immortals, many-named, for aye
Almighty, Lord of all things, who dost sway
   The world with ordered governance, all hail!
Thou God, to whom of right all mortals pray.

From Thee we have our being, and the dower
Of speech, alone of things that live their hour
   And move on earth : for this my chant to
      Thee
Shall rise, and I will ever sing Thy power.

For Thee this universe revolveth still
About our earth, obedient to Thy will ;
   Even as Thou guidest ordering its course,
And Thy behest with gladness doth fulfil.

ΚΛΕΑΝΘΗΣ

τοῖον ἔχεις ὑποεργὸν ἀκινήτοις ἐνὶ χερσίν
ἀμφήκη πυρόεντα ἀεὶ ζώοντα κεραυνόν,
τοῦ γὰρ ὑπὸ πληγῆς φύσεως πάντ' ἐρρί-
γασιν,   .
ᾧ σὺ κατευθύνεις κοινὸν λόγον, ὃς διὰ
πάντων
φοιτᾷ μιγνύμενος μεγάλοις μικροῖς τε
φάεσσιν,
ὃς τόσσος γεγαὼς ὕπατος βασιλεὺς διὰ
παντός.
οὐδέ τι γίγνεται ἔργον ἐπὶ χθονὶ σοῦ
δίχα, δαῖμον,
οὔτε κατ' αἰθέριον θεῖον πόλον, οὔτ' ἐπὶ
πόντῳ,
πλὴν ὁπόσα ῥέζουσι κακοὶ σφετέρῃσιν
ἀνοίαις.

So strong a servant hast Thou of Thine aim,
Grasped in Thy hands invincible, the flame
  Of the forked ever-living lightning flash,
Beneath whose stroke shudders all Nature's
  frame ;

Wherewith Thou dost direct the common
  Word
That ever passing through all things is heard,
  Mingling with greater as with lesser lights ;
And being so mighty, everywhere art Lord.

Without Thee, Spirit, there is nothing wrought
On earth, in air the heavenly region nought,
  Upon the waters nothing—save the wrongs
The wicked work, by foolishness distraught.

M. VALERIVS MARTIALIS

PUELLA senibus dulcior mihi
cygnis,
agna Galesi mollior Phalantini,
concha Lucrini delicatior stagni ;
cui nec lapillos praeferas Ery-
thraeos
nec modo politum pecudis In-
dicae dentem,
niuesque primas, liliumque non
tactum ;
quae crine uicit Baetici gregis
uellus,
Rhenique nodos, aureamque nite-
lam ;

THE DEAD CHILD

LITTLE maiden, sweeter far to me
  Than the swans are with their vaunted
    snows,
Maid more tender than the lambkins be
  Where Galesus by Phalantus flows ;

Daintier than daintiest shells that lie
  By the ripples of the Lucrine wave ;
Choicer than new-polished ivory
  That the herds from Indian jungles gave ;

Choicer than Erythrae's marbles white,
  Snows new-fallen, lilies yet unsoiled :
Softer were your tresses and more bright
  Than the locks by German maidens coiled,

fragrauit ore, quod rosarium Paesti,
quod Atticarum prima mella cerarum,
quod succinorum rapta de manu gleba,
cui comparatus indecens erat pauo,
inamabilis sciurus, et frequens Phoenix ;
adhuc repenti tepet Erotion busto,
quam pessimorum lex auara Fatorum
sexta peregit hieme, nec tamen tota.
Nostros amores, gaudiumque, lususque.

v. 37.

THE DEAD CHILD

Than the finest fleeces Baetis shows,
   Than the dormouse with her golden hue :
Lips more fragrant than the Paestan rose,
   Than the Attic bees' first honey-dew,

Or an amber ball, new-pressed and warm ;
   Paled the peacock's sheen, in your compare ;
E'en the winsome squirrel lost his charm,
   And the Phoenix seemed no longer rare.

Scarce Erotion's ashes yet are cold ;
   Greedily grim fate ordained to smite
Ere her sixth brief winter had grown old—
   Little love, my bliss, my heart's delight.

ΑΡΙΣΤΟΦΑΝΗΣ

εὐλογῆσαι βουλόμεσθα τοὺς πατέρας
    ἡμῶν, ὅτι
ἄνδρες ἦσαν τῆσδε τῆς γῆς ἄξιοι καὶ
    τοῦ πέπλου,
οἵτινες πέζαις μάχαισιν ἔν τε ναυ-
    φάρκτῳ στρατῷ
πανταχοῦ νικῶντες ἀεὶ τήνδ' ἐκόσ-
    μησαν πόλιν·
οὐ γὰρ οὐδεὶς πώποτ' αὐτῶν τοὺς
    ἐναντίους ἰδὼν
ἠρίθμησεν, ἀλλ' ὁ θυμὸς εὐθὺς ἦν
    ἀμυνίας·
εἰ δέ που πέσοιεν ἐς τὸν ὠμὸν ἐν
    μάχῃ τινί,
τοῦτ' ἀπεψήσαντ' ἂν, εἶτ' ἠρνοῦντο
    μὴ πεπτωκέναι

36

THE GOOD OLD TIMES

SING we the praise of our fathers to-day ;
Worthy the land and the Mantle were
they :
Warriors battling afloat or ashore,
Everywhere triumphing, still winning
more
Fame for the City.   When facing the
foe,
Never a man of them counted them—
No !
Valour was straightway in arms and
a-fire.
Did one in fighting fall flat in the
mire ?
Brush off the mud, never own to the
fall !

ΑΡΙΣΤΟΦΑΝΗΣ

ἀλλὰ διεπάλαιον αὖθις. καὶ στρατη-
γὸς οὐδ' ἂν εἷς
τῶν πρὸ τοῦ σίτησιν ᾔτησ' ἐρόμενος
Κλεαίνετον·
νῦν δ' ἐὰν μὴ προεδρίαν φέρωσι καὶ
τὰ σιτία,
οὐ μαχεῖσθαί φασιν. ἡμεῖς δ' ἀξιοῦ-
μεν τῇ πόλει
προῖκα γενναίως ἀμύνειν καὶ θεοῖς
ἐγχωρίοις.
καὶ πρὸς οὐκ αἰτοῦμεν οὐδὲν, πλὴν
τοσουτονὶ μόνον·
ἤν ποτ' εἰρήνη γένηται καὶ πόνων
παυσώμεθα,
μὴ φθονεῖθ' ἡμῖν κομῶσι μηδ' ἀπεσ-
τλεγγισμένοις.

EQUITES, 565.

38

Back to the grip! not a man of them all
Chosen for Captain would clamour for
  feeding,
Beg of Cleaenetus. Now, they're all
  needing
Victuals as well as precedence—if not,
They won't go fighting, this valorous
  lot!
Ah, but we count it for glory to guard
Nobly and well, for no dirty reward,
Altar and home; and no guerdon beside
Ask, but this only—if peace shall betide,
Labours be ended, don't grudge if we
  wear
Love-locks, and sport quite a dandified
  air.

ΕΥΡΙΠΙΔΗΣ

ὦ φίλταθ᾽ ὥς σοι θάνατος ἦλθε δυστυχής.

εἰ μὲν γὰρ ἔθανες πρὸ πόλεως, ἥβης
τυχὼν

γάμων τε καὶ τῆς ἰσοθέου τυραννίδος,

μακάριος ἦσθ᾽ ἄν, εἴ τι τῶνδε μακάριον.

νῦν δ᾽ αὖτ᾽ ἰδὼν μὲν γνούς τε τῇ ψυχῇ,
τέκνον,

οὐκ οἶσθ᾽, ἐχρήσω δ᾽ οὐδὲν ἐν δόμοις
ἔχων.

δύστηνε, κρατὸς ὥς σ᾽ ἔκειρεν ἀθλίως

τείχη πατρῷα, Λοξίου πυργώματα,

ὃν πόλλ᾽ ἐκήπευσ᾽ ἡ τεκοῦσα βόστρυχον

φιλήμασίν τ᾽ ἔδωκεν, ἔνθεν ἐκγελᾷ

ὀστέων ῥαγέντων φόνος, ἵν᾽ αἰσχρὰ μὴ
λέγω.

40

ASTYANAX

OH, it was hard, so hard for thee to die,
My darling.   To have fallen before the walls
In manhood's vigour, having known the joys
Of wedlock, lived a king the mate of gods—
Why, that were happiness, if ought there be
Of happiness in the world.   But now, poor babe,
Thou didst behold these things, and learn of
     them,
But know them never, never at all could'st taste
Possession of them in a home thine own.
Unhappy ! how thy fathers' walls, the towers
Of Loxias, have piteously laid low
The curls thy mother tended oft and kissed—
Whence grins a carnage now of shattered bones,
And worse I will not name.

ΕΥΡΙΠΙΔΗΣ

ὦ χεῖρες, ὡς εἰκοὺς μὲν ἡδείας πατρὸς
κέκτησθ᾽, ἐν ἄρθροις δ᾽ ἔκλυτοι πρόκεισθέ
    μοι.
ὦ πολλὰ κόμπους ἐκβαλόν φίλον στόμα,
ὄλωλας, ἐψεύσω μ᾽, ὅτ᾽ εἰσπίπτων λέχος,
ὦ μῆτερ, ηὔδας, ᾖ πολύν σοι βοστρύχων
πλόκαμον κεροῦμαι πρὸς τάφον θ᾽ ὁμηλί-
    κων
κώμους ἀπάξω, φίλα διδοὺς προσφθέγματα.
σὺ δ᾽ οὐκ ἔμ᾽, ἀλλ᾽ ἐγὼ σὲ τὸν νεώτερον
γραῦς ἄπολις ἄτεκνος ἄθλιον θάπτω νε-
    κρόν.
οἴμοι, τὰ πόλλ᾽ ἀσπάσμαθ᾽ αἵ τ᾽ ἐμαὶ τροφαὶ
πόνοι τ᾽ ἐκεῖνοι φροῦδά μοι. τί καί ποτε
γράψειεν ἂν σῷ μουσοποιὸς ἐν τάφῳ;
τὸν παῖδα τόνδ᾽ ἔκτειναν Ἀργεῖοί ποτε
δείσαντες; αἰσχρὸν τοὐπίγραμμά γ᾽ Ἑλ-
    λάδι.

TROADES, 1167.

42

Ah, little hands,
So sweet a counterfeit of his, thy sire's,
Nerveless before me droop your fingers now.
Ah, little lips that prattled boastfully,
Ye are dumb, ye played me false, when on my
　　couch
Thou once didst fling thyself, and cry, 'Oh,
　　mother,
The plenteous locks I'll cut me off, and bring
My comrades to your tomb in companies,
With loving words!'—Not thou, not thou for me,
But I for thee,—a homeless, childless crone,
For thee, so young,—prepare the untimely grave.
Ah me, the fond caresses, all the care
And all the loving labour, gone, all gone!
What should a poet write upon thy tomb?
'This boy the Argives slew,—because they
　　feared!'
Black, black the shame to Hellas of that rede.

SEX. AVRELIVS PROPERTIVS

QUANDOCUNQUE igitur nostros
mors claudet ocellos,
accipe quae serues funeris acta
mei.

Nec mea tunc longa spatietur ima-
gine pompa,
nec tuba sit fati uana querela
mei,

nec mihi tunc fulcro sternatur lectus
eburno,
nec sit in Attalico mors mea nixa
toro.

THE POET'S DEATH

AND so whene'er it shall befall
That with shut eyes in death I sleep,
Hear now the rites thy care shall keep,
The service of my funeral.

The slow procession shall not wend
With waxen masks, an endless show ;
For me the trumpet shall not blow,
Vain wailing for the destined end.

Let not the couch for me that day
Be spread upon an ivory frame ;
Not such as Attalus might claim,
The bed whereon my corpse you lay.

45

Desit odoriferis ordo mihi lancibus,
   adsint
plebei paruae funeris exequiae.

Sat mihi sat magna est si tres sint
   pompa libelli,
   quos ego Persephonae maxima dona
   feram.

Tu uero nudum pectus lacerata
   sequeris,
   nec fueris nomen lassa uocare
   meum,

osculaque in gelidis pones suprema
   labellis,
   cum dabitur Syrio munere plenus
   onyx.

THE POET'S DEATH

No savours sweet from platters rare
  For me in ordered state shall rise ;
  The rites that mark my obsequies
Be those that lowly folk may share.

Enough of pomp, enough for me,
  These three slight books of mine to take—
  The richest gift that I can make
For homage to Persephone.

But thou, but thou behind wilt press,
  And smite in grief thy bosom bare ;
  Nor ever wilt thou tire nor spare
To call my name for weariness.

And thou wilt print thy kiss, the last
  Long kiss on lips that death has chilled,
  When with its Syrian treasure filled
The onyx casket down is cast.

Deinde, ubi suppositus cinerem me fecerit
   ardor,
   accipiat manes paruola testa meos,

et sit in exiguo laurus super addita
   busto
   quae tegat extincti funeris umbra
   locum ;

et duo sint versus, 'qui nunc iacet
   horrida puluis,
   unius hic quondam seruus amoris
   erat.'

                     iii. 5.

And when at length the kindled flame
  My body shall to ashes burn,
  An earthen vase, a tiny urn,
Shall hold the ghost that bore my name.

And on the scanty plot shall grow
  A laurel, where had stood my pyre,
  And cast its shadows where the fire
Of death long since has ceased to glow.

And brief my epitaph shall run :
  ' While yet he lived, who now is just
  This handful of unlovely dust,
One love he served, and served but one.'

D

ΑΡΙΣΤΟΦΑΝΗΣ

ὦ σοφώτατοι θεαταὶ, δεῦρο τὸν νοῦν
πρόσεχετε.
ἠδικημέναι γὰρ ὑμῖν μεμφόμεσθ᾽ ἐν
ἄντιον.
πλεῖστα γὰρ θεῶν ἁπάντων ὠφελοί-
σαις τὴν πόλιν,
δαιμόνων ἡμῖν μόναις οὐ θύετ᾽ οὐδὲ
σπένδετε,
αἵτινες τηροῦμεν ὑμᾶς. ἢν γὰρ ᾖ τις
ἔξοδος
μηδενὶ ξὺν νῷ, τότ᾽ ἢ βροντῶμεν ἢ
ψακάζομεν.
εἶτα τὸν θεοῖσιν ἐχθρὸν βυρσοδέψην
Παφλαγόνα

50

THE REPROOF

JUDICIOUS spectators! attention we pray.
We are hurt, and we 've something reproachful
   to say.
Not a god of them all gives more help to the
   nation,
Yet never an offering, ne'er a libation
Comes our way—just ours, who look after you so.
Why, whene'er on some cracked expedition
   you go,
We thunder or drizzle.   As every one knows,
When that damned Paphlagonian tanner you
   chose
For your Captain, black brows we drew down
   and we scowled,

ἡνίχ' ἡρεῖσθε στρατηγὸν, τὰς ὀφρῦς
συνήγομεν
κἀποιοῦμεν δεινά· βροντὴ δ' ἐρράγη
δι' ἀστραπῆς·
ἡ σελήνη δ' ἐξέλειπε τὰς ὅδους· ὁ δ'
ἥλιος
τὴν θρυαλλίδ' εἰς ἑαυτὸν εὐθέως
συνελκύσας
οὐ φανεῖν ἔφασκεν ὑμῖν, εἰ στρατη-
γήσει Κλέων.
ἀλλ' ὅμως εἵλεσθε τοῦτον. φασὶ γὰρ
δυσβουλίαν
τῇδε τῇ πόλει προσεῖναι, ταῦτα μέντοι
τοὺς θεοὺς
ἅττ' ἂν ὑμεῖς ἐξαμάρτητ' ἐπὶ τὸ
βέλτιον τρέπειν.
ὡς δὲ καὶ τοῦτο ξυνοίσει ῥᾳδίως
διδάξομεν.
ἢν Κλέωνα τὸν λάρον δώρων ἑλόντες
καὶ κλοπῆς,

And made an appalling to-do : thunder
    howled,
Lightning blazed ; the moon slid from her
    natural way,
And the sun drew his wick in, and vowed
    ' not a ray
Shall be granted if Cleon be Captain,' and
    still
You elected just him.   Well, when counsels
    of ill
Possess you, they say that, whatever
    befall,
The gods turn your blunders to luck after
    all.
Now we'll tell in a word how to turn this
    to healing ;
If only this cormorant of borrowing and
    stealing,
This Cleon you seize, and if promptly you
    stock him,

εἶτα φιμώσητε τούτου τῷ ξύλῳ τὸν
αὐχένα,
αὖθις εἰς τἀρχαῖον ὑμῖν, εἴ τι κἀζη-
μάρτετε,
ἐπὶ τὸ βέλτιον τὸ πρᾶγμα τῇ πόλει
συνοίσεται.

NUBES, 575.

If fast in the pillory collared you lock
him,
In spite of your small aberration, once
more
The affair will bring luck to the State, as
before.

ΑΙΣΧΥΛΟΣ

ΧΟ. καὶ τίς τόδ᾽ ἐξίκοιτ᾽ ἂν ἀγγέλων
τάχος;

ΚΛ. Ἥφαιστος, Ἴδης λαμπρὸν ἐκπέμπων
σέλας.

φρυκτὸς δὲ φρυκτὸν δεῦρ᾽ ἀπ᾽ ἀγγάρου
πυρὸς

ἔπεμπεν. Ἴδη μὲν πρὸς Ἑρμαῖον
λέπας

Λήμνου· μέγαν δὲ πανὸν ἐκ νήσου
τρίτον

Ἄθωον αἶπος Ζηνὸς ἐξεδέξατο

ὑπερτελής τε (πόντον ὥστε νωτίσαι,

ἰσχὺς πορευτοῦ λαμπάδος πρὸς ἡδο-
νὴν)

THE BEACON-RACE

Cɪɪ. Yea? But what messenger could speed
so fast?

CLYT. The Fire-god, flaming bright on Ida's
crest ;
Beacon to beacon flashed the courier-
blaze—
Ida to Hermes' Crag in Lemnos isle :
And the great island bonfire, Athos Point
The mount of Zeus the third in order
caught,
And, towering high to skim the watery
waste
It fed the speeding glare with joyous
strength—

πεύκη, τὸ χρυσοφεγγὲς ὥς τις ἥλιος
σέλας παραγγείλασα Μακίστου σκοπάς·
ὃ δ' οὔτι μέλλων οὐδ' ἀφρασμόνως ὕπνῳ
νικώμενος παρῆκεν ἀγγέλου μέρος·
ἑκὰς δὲ φρυκτοῦ φῶς ἐπ' Εὐρίπου
    ῥοὰς
Μεσσαπίου φύλαξι σημαίνει μολόν.
οἱ δ' ἀντέλαμψαν καὶ παρήγγειλαν
    πρόσω
γραίας ἐρείκης θωμὸν ἅψαντες πυρί.
σθένουσα λαμπὰς δ' οὐδέπω μαυρου-
    μένη
·ὑπερθοροῦσα πεδίον Ἀσωποῦ, δίκην
φαιδρᾶς σελήνης, πρὸς Κιθαιρῶνος λέ-
    πας
ἤγειρεν ἄλλην ἐκδοχὴν πομποῦ πυρός.
φάος δὲ τηλέπομπον οὐκ ἠναίνετο
φρουρά, πλέον καίουσα τῶν εἰρημένων·
λίμνην δ' ὑπὲρ Γοργῶπιν ἔσκηψεν
    φάος·

A shining brand, that tossed the golden
    beam
Sun-like to a watcher on Macistus height.
Nor tarried he, nor failed to play his part
Of messenger, o'ercome by heedless sleep.
To far Euripus' streams the beacon light
Shot with its signal to Messapius' guards:
Their answering fire still flashed the tidings
    on,
Who set the high-piled heather sere ablaze;
The mighty torch, unflagging, leaped the
    plain
Of far Asopus, like a gleaming moon,
On to Cithaeron's rock, and roused once
    more
A fresh successor of the news-fraught flare.
Nor did the watch their herald-flame deny,
But more than bidden heaped the warning
    glow.
Across the mere Gorgopis flashed the light,

ὄρος τ' ἐπ' Αἰγίπλαγκτον ἐξικνούμενον
ὤτρυνε θεσμὸν μὴ χαρίζεσθαι πυρός.
πέμπουσι δ' ἀνδαίοντες ἀφθόνῳ μένει
φλογὸς μέγαν πώγωνα, καὶ Σαρωνικοῦ
πορθμοῦ κάτοπτον πρῶν' ὑπερβάλλειν
    πρόσω
φλέγουσαν· εἶτ' ἔσκηψεν, εἶτ' ἀφίκετο
'Αραχναῖον αἶπος, ἀστυγείτονας σκο-
    πάς·
κἄπειτ' 'Ατρειδῶν ἐς τό γε σκήπτει
    στέγος
φάος τόδ' οὐκ ἄπαππον 'Ιδαίου πυρός.
τοιοίδε τοί μοι λαμπαδηφόρων νόμοι,
ἄλλος παρ' ἄλλου διαδοχαῖς πληρού-
    μενοι·
νικᾷ δ' ὁ πρῶτος καὶ τελευταῖος δρα-
    μών.
τέκμαρ τοιοῦτον σύμβολόν τέ σοι λέγω
ἀνδρὸς παραγγείλαντος ἐκ Τροίας ἐμοί.

AGAMEMNON, 292.

Reached Aegiplanctus, stirred them rous-
ingly
In nowise to neglect the fires ordained.
They kindle and send on with strength
undimmed
A giant beard of blaze, whose beams o'er-
leaped
The cliff that frowns on the Saronic strait.
Then, then, it darted, then at length
attained
Arachne's crag, the post hard by our town :
So lighted last here on our royal roof
The fiery heir of Ida's flame begot.
Such was the ordering of my torch-bearers,
Making the course complete, each after each ;
And the first wins, though hindmost in the
race.
Such token and such sign to you I tell,
As such to me my lord hath sent from Troy.

P. VERGILIVS MARO

TENE, inquit, miserande puer, cum laeta
   ueniret,
inuidit Fortuna mihi, ne regna uideres
nostra, neque ad sedes uictor ueherere
   paternas?
non haec Euandro de te promissa parenti
discedens dederam ; cum me complexus
   euntem
mitteret in magnum imperium, metu-
   ensque moneret
acres esse uiros, cum dura proelia gente.
At nunc ille quidem spe multum captus
   inani
fors et uota facit, cumulatque altaria
   donis:

PALLAS DEAD

'AH, luckless youth! when Fortune came in glee,
  Was it to grudge me thee, that thou shouldst
    ne'er
Behold my kingship, nor in victory
  Triumphant to thy father's halls repair?
  Not this the parting promise that I sware
To Evander thy old sire, when he embraced me,
With anxious warnings, how the foe that faced
    me

' Is fierce, and stern the race with whom I cope ;
  So sent me forth to win wide empery.
He sorely now beguiled with empty hope
  Perchance makes offering, piles the altars high
  With many a gift ; while we right mournfully

nos iuuenem exanimum, et nil iam
caelestibus ullis

debentem uano maesti comitamur
honore.

Infelix, nati funus crudele uidebis.

Hi nostri reditus,exspectatique triumphi?

Haec mea magna fides? At non Euandre
pudendis

uolneribus pulsum aspicies, nec sospite
dirum

optabis nato funus pater. Hei mihi,
quantum

praesidium Ausonia, et quantum tu
perdis, Iule.

Haec ubi defleuit, tolli miserabile
corpus

imperat, et toto lectos ex agmine mittit

mille uiros, qui supremum comitentur
honorem

intersintque patris lacrimis, solatia
luctus

With honours vain his lifeless son escort,
His debt discharged to all the heavenly court.

' Thou shalt but see thy son's most cruel lot.
  Is this our coming? this the victor's prize?
This my high troth?   But not, Evander, not
    Stricken with shameful wounds he meets thine
      eyes,
    Nor for a sterner doom the father cries,
The son unharmed. How dear a guard is gone
For thee, Ausonia, and for thee, my son!'

With tears Aeneas ended : then commands
  To be uplifted high the lifeless frame ;
Picked from the hosts he sends the chosen bands,
  A thousand warriors : who to guard him came,
  And pay the last sad honours to his name,
And share the father's tears—a scant relief
To that sad father due, for boundless grief.

exigua ingentis, misero sed debita patri.
Haud segnes alii crates et molle feretrum
arbuteis texunt uirgis et uimine querno,
extructosque toros obtentu frondis inum-
 brant.
Hic iuuenem agresti sublimem stramine
 ponunt :
qualem uirgineo demissum pollice florem,
seu mollis uiolae, seu languentis hya-
 cinthi,
cui neque fulgor adhuc, nec iam sua
 forma recessit :
non iam mater alit tellus, uiresque mini-
 strat.

AENEID, xi. 42

PALLAS DEAD

Some with swift hands a wicker frame enlace,
A pliant litter, of the saplings twined
Of arbutus and shoots of oak : and place
  O'ershadowing leaves ; whose verdure all
    enshrined
The funeral bed thus cunningly designed.
Then on the couch in woodland guise arrayed
On high the corse of that sweet youth is laid.

Even such he seemed, as some fair flower that
    fell
  By maiden fingers plucked and laid full low,
Some tender violet, or some drooping bell
  Of the blue hyacinth ; the living glow
  Still lingers—still the delicate grace ye know.
No more the earth her child may feed with dew,
Nor that young life that filled its veins renew.

ΑΡΙΣΤΟΦΑΝΗΣ

πολλάκις γ' ἡμῖν ἔδοξεν ἡ πόλις πεπον-
θέναι
ταυτὸν ἔς τε τῶν πολιτῶν τοὺς καλούς τε
κἀγαθοὺς
ἔς τε τἀρχαῖον νόμισμα καὶ τὸ καινὸν
χρυσίον.
οἵτε γὰρ τούτοισιν οὖσιν οὐ κεκιβδηλευ-
μένοις,
ἀλλὰ καλλίστοις ἁπάντων, ὡς δοκεῖ, νομισ-
μάτων,
καὶ μόνοις ὀρθῶς κοπεῖσι καὶ κεκωδωνισ-
μένοις
ἔν τε τοῖς Ἕλλησι καὶ τοῖς βαρβάροισι
πανταχοῦ,

68

COUNTERFEIT COINS

Now the thought has often struck me that
  our conduct is the same
In the matter of our citizens who bear an
  honoured name,
As in dealing with the coins of olden
  mintage and the new.
These, which no alloy debases, coins without a peer—it's true—
None so perfect in the cutting, none like
  these that ring so sound,
Search through all the lands of Hellas, all
  the strangers' realms around—

χρύμεθ' οὐδὲν, ἀλλὰ τούτοις τοῖς πονηροῖς
  χαλκίοις
χθές τε καὶ πρώην κοπεῖσι τῷ κακίστῳ
  κόμματι,
τῶν πολιτῶν θ' οὓς μὲν ἴσμεν εὐγενεῖς καὶ
  σώφρονας
ἄνδρας ὄντας καὶ δικαίους καὶ καλούς τε
  κἀγαθούς,
καὶ τραφέντας ἐν παλαίστραις καὶ χοροῖς
  καὶ μουσικῇ,
προυσελοῦμεν, τοῖς δὲ χαλκοῖς καὶ ξένοις
  καὶ πυρρίαις
καὶ πονηροῖς κἀκ πονηρῶν εἰς ἅπαντα
  χρώμεθα
ὑστάτοις ἀφιγμένοισιν, οἷσιν ἡ πόλις πρὸ
  τοῦ
οὐδέ φαρμακοῖσιν εἰκῆ ῥᾳδίως ἐχρήσατ'
  ἄν.
ἀλλὰ καὶ νῦν, ὦνόητοι, μεταβαλόντες τοὺς
  τρόπους,

These we never use, preferring the atrocious
   brassy crew
Cut just now or t'other morning—cut so
   very vilely, too !
So whene'er we know a citizen is nobly
   born and sensible,
A man of truth and honour trained in
   sports and arts and graces,
We insult him, and some foreign scamp,
   some brazen slave ostensible,
Some blackguard born of blackguard stock,
   we plant in all the 'places' :
All the very last arrivals we'd have felt
   some hesitation
Long ago in even sacrificing rashly for the
   nation.
Come, e'en now, you'd best reform, my
   foolish friends, and change your ways,
Use again the useful folks. If you succeed,
   it's only just ;

ΑΡΙΣΤΟΦΑΝΗΣ

χρῆσθε τοῖς χρηστοῖσιν αἶθις· καὶ κατ-
   ορθώσασι γὰρ
εὔλογον· κἄν τι σφαλῆτ', ἐξ ἀξίου γοῖν
   τοῦ ξύλου,
ἤν τι καὶ πάσχητε, πάσχειν τοῖς σοφοῖς
   δοκήσετε.

RANAE, 718.

COUNTERFEIT COINS

And if still you fail and come to grief, yet
    every wise man says
You've a gallows worth the hanging from,
    at least, if hang you must!

ΕΥΡΙΠΙΔΗΣ

ΑΔ. φίλοι, γυναικὸς δαίμον᾽ εὐτυχέστερον
τοὐμοῦ νομίζω, καίπερ οὐ δοκοῦνθ᾽ ὅμως·
τῆς μὲν γὰρ οὐδὲν ἄλγος ἅψεταί ποτε
πολλῶν δὲ μόχθων εὐκλεὴς ἐπαύσατο.
ἐγὼ δ᾽ ὃν οὐ χρῆν ζῆν, παρεὶς τὸ μόρσι-
μον
λυπρὸν διάξω βίοτον· ἄρτι μανθάνω.
πῶς γὰρ δόμων τῶνδ᾽ εἰσόδους ἀνέξομαι;
τίν᾽ ἂν προσειπών, τοῦ δὲ προσρηθεὶς ὕπο,
τερπνῆς τύχοιμ᾽ ἂν εἰσόδου; ποῖ τρέψο-
μαι;
ἡ μὲν γὰρ ἔνδον ἐξελᾷ μ᾽ ἐρημία,
γυναικὸς εὐνὰς εὖτ᾽ ἂν εἰσίδω κενὰς
θρόνους τ᾽ ἐν οἷσιν ἷζε, καὶ κατὰ στέγας

ADMETUS

Ah, friends, I hold my wife's the happier lot,
Happier than mine, for all it seems not so.
Her shall no pain touch any more ; the praise
Is hers, who found release from many a grief.
But I, who should not live, gave fate the slip,
And must to the end drag out a dreary life.
I see it now ; it breaks upon me now.
How shall I bear home-coming—to this home ?
Whom shall I greet, or who will greet me back,
To cheer that coming home ?   Where shall I
        turn ?
Indoors, the desolateness will drive me forth,
Whene'er I look upon her empty couch,
Her empty chair where she was wont to sit,
The dusty floors that lack her woman's care ;

75

ΕΥΡΙΠΙΔΗΣ

αὐχμηρὸν οὖδας, τέκνα δ᾽ ἀμφὶ γούνασι
πίπτοντα κλαίῃ μητέρ᾽, οἱ δὲ δεσπότιν
στένωσιν οἵαν ἐκ δόμων ἀπώλεσαν.
τὰ μὲν κατ᾽ οἴκους τοιάδ᾽· ἔξωθεν
    δέ με
γάμοι τ᾽ ἐλῶσι Θεσσαλῶν καὶ ξύλλογοι
γυναικοπληθεῖς· οὐ γὰρ ἐξανέξομαι
λεύσσων δάμαρτος τῆς ἐμῆς ὁμήλικας.
ἐρεῖ δέ μ᾽ ὅστις ἐχθρὸς ὢν κυρεῖ τάδε·
ἰδοῦ τὸν αἰσχρῶς ζῶνθ᾽, ὃς οὐκ ἔτλη
    θανεῖν,
ἀλλ᾽ ἣν ἔγημεν ἀντιδοὺς ἀψυχίᾳ
πέφευγεν Ἅιδην· κᾆτ᾽ ἀνὴρ εἶναι δοκεῖ;
στυγεῖ δὲ τοὺς τεκόντας, αὐτὸς οἱ
    θέλων
θανεῖν. τοιάνδε πρὸς κακοῖσι κληδόνα
ἕξω. τί μοι ζῆν δῆτα κύδιον, φίλοι,
κακῶς κλύοντι καὶ κακῶς πεπραγότι;

ALCESTIS, 935.

ADMETUS

Whene'er the children cling about my knees,
Sobbing out 'Mother! mother!' and the folk
Bewail the wise sweet mistress they have lost.
So will it be within : and out of doors,
The people's wedding feasts, the gatherings
Where women throng, will drive me thence again.
For never shall I dare to see the face
Of dames whose years were matched with hers,
    my wife's.
And every man that bears me hard will say,
'Lo there! the wretch whose life is a reproach,
Who dared not die, but, for his coward soul,
Yielded his wedded wife in his own stead,
So balked his doom ! And count you this a man?
He hates his very parents, for his dread
Of his own dying.'   Other ills beside,
This is the vile repute that must be mine.
How then is life for me more enviable
With darkened name and fame, and darkened
    days ?

Q. HORATIVS FLACCVS

NON ebur neque aureum
mea renidet in domo lacunar,
non trabes Hymettiae
premunt columnas ultima re-
cisas
Africa, neque Attali
ignotus heres regiam occupaui,
nec Laconicas mihi
trahunt honestae purpuras cli-
entae.
At fides et ingeni
benigna uena est, pauperemque
diues
me petit ; nihil supra

THE VANITY OF RICHES

GOLDEN ceilings, ivory fine,
Do not grace this home of mine;
Marbles from Hymettus brought
Press not upon pillars wrought
Out of Afric's quarries far:
Not for me the splendours are
Of halls for Attalus erected
(Proved an heir all unsuspected!)
No good spinners for me ply
Threads Laconian purples dye.
Loyal heart and kindly wit
To rich guests a welcome fit
Yield, tho' I the host be poor.
Nothing ampler I implore

deos lacesso nec potentem
    amicum
largiora flagito
satis beatus unicis Sabinis.
Truditur dies die
nouaeque pergunt interire
    lunae.
Tu secanda marmora
locas sub ipsum funus et
    sepulcri
immemor struis domos,
marisque Baiis obstrepentis
    urgues
summouere litora,
parum locuples continente ripa.
Quid quod usque proximos
reuellis agri terminos et ultra
limites clientium
salis auarus? Pellitur pater-
    nos

Of the gods, importunate;
Nor from friendship with the great
Seek to win a richer prize:
Since my Sabine farm supplies
Bliss enough for all my needs.
Day to fleeting day succeeds;
Still the new moons wax and wane
Till their light is gone again.
You contract for marbled floors—
Death is knocking at your doors.
Thoughtless of your tomb, you pile
Palaces, and strive awhile
To extend your barriered shore
Where the seas of Baiae roar,
Since the beach that bounds the waves
Fails of what your lacking craves.
Nay, you pluck the landmarks out
Of the neighbouring fields about;
Skip the clients' borders o er,
Lightly—yearning yet for more.

in sinu ferens deos
et uxor et uir sordidosque
     natos.
Nulla certior tamen
rapacis Orci fine destinata
aula diuitem manet
erum.   Quid ultra tendis?
     Aequa tellus
pauperi recluditur
regumque pueris, nec satelles
     Orci
callidum Promethea
reuexit auro captus.   Hic
     superbum
Tantalum atque Tantali
genus coercet, hic leuare
     functum
pauperem laboribus
uocatus atque non uocatus
     audit.

ODES, ii. 18

Wife and husband forth are thrust ;
In their arms they carry just
Gods their fathers honoured aye,
And their babes—to poverty.
Yet, though rich the owner be,
Ne'er a house so certainly
Waits him as the one decreed
By devouring Orcus' meed.
Would you pass the limit set ?
Prince and pauper, equal yet
Is the space for each prepared :
Nor by golden bribes ensnared
Did His ferryman restore
Over-wise Prometheus o'er.
Tantalus, for all his pride,
Him and all his race beside
He constraineth ; and 'tis He
Hears the poor man's litany
Craving rest from toil and tears—
Called or no, 'tis Orcus hears.

ΕΥΡΙΠΙΔΗΣ

ὅταν δὲ βορέας χιόνα Θρήκιος χέῃ,
δ'ραισι θηρᾶν σῶμα περιβαλὼν ἔμον,
καὶ πῦρ ἀναίθων, χιόνος οὐδέν μοι
  μέλει.
ἡ γῆ δ' ἀνάγκῃ κᾶν θέλῃ κᾶν μὴ
  θέλῃ
τίκτουσα ποίαν τἀμὰ πιαίνει βοτά.
ἀγὼ οὔτινι θύω πλὴν ἐμοί, θεοῖσι δ'
  οὔ,
καὶ τῇ μεγίστῃ γαστρὶ τῇδε δαιμόνων.
ὡς τοὔμπιεῖν γε καὶ φαγεῖν τοὔφ'
  ἡμέραν,
Ζεῦς οὗτος ἀνθρώποισι τοῖσι σώφροσι,

THE CYCLOPEAN PHILOSOPHY

WHEN the North wind from Thrace brings
    the snows up,
In the skins of wild beasts I wrap close up,
Poke the fire well, and care not a stiver
For the storm. And the Earth must be giver
Willy-nilly of plentiful grazing
To fatten the cattle I'm raising.
To myself I pay sacrifice solely,
Not to one of your gods—no such folly—
And my belly, the best (as you see it is)
And biggest of all the deities.
To eat all the day, and to tipple,
That's Zeus to all sensible people ;

ΕΥΡΙΠΙΔΗΣ

λυπεῖν δὲ μηδὲν αὐτόν· οἳ δὲ τοὶς νόμους
ἔθεντο, ποικίλλοντες ἀνθρώπων βίον,
κλαίειν ἄνωγα· τὴν δ' ἐμὴν ψυχὴν ἐγὼ
οἳ παύσομαι δρῶν εἶ κατεσθίων τε σέ.

CYCLOPS, 329.

THE CYCLOPEAN PHILOSOPHY

And never let anything vex you.
The folk that make laws, and perplex you
With making a man's life a pother—
Be hanged to their meddling and bother.
For myself, I 'll continue to treat you
As best suits myself—and to eat you.

ΕΥΡΙΠΙΔΗΣ

ΜΑ. ὦ χαῖρε, πρέσβυ, χαῖρε, καὶ δίδασκε μοι
τοιούσδε τούσδε παῖδας, ἐς τὸ πᾶν σοφούς,
ὥσπερ σύ· μηδὲν μᾶλλον· ἀρκέσουσι γάρ.
πειρῶ δὲ σῶσαι μὴ θανεῖν πρόθυμος ὤν·
σοὶ παῖδές ἐσμεν· σαῖν χεροῖν τεθράμ-
μεθα.
ὁρᾷς δὲ κἀμὲ τὴν ἐμὴν ὥραν γάμου
διδοῦσαν ἀντὶ τῶνδε κατθανουμένην.
ὑμεῖς τ᾽ ἀδελφῶν ἡ παροῦσ᾽ ὁμιλία
εὐδαιμονοῖτε, καὶ γένοιθ᾽ ὑμῖν ὅσων
ἡ ᾽μὴ πάροιθεν καρδία σφαλήσεται.
καὶ τὸν γέροντα τήν τ᾽ ἔσω γραῖαν
δόμων

THE SACRIFICE

FAREWELL, old friend, farewell. For these my
 brothers,
Train them for my sake like thyself, in all
Wise, as thou art ; no more ; sufficeth so.
Strive to deliver them from death, kind heart—
Thy children are we, nurselings of thy hands.
I too, thou seest, can give my bridal bloom
For them, for their sakes shall go forth to die.
 And you, my band of brothers, round me now,
All happiness be yours, yours all the bliss
Whereof too soon my heart shall be bereft.
Honour this aged man beside ; and her
The old dame within, Alcmene, she that bore

ΕΥΡΙΠΙΔΗΣ

τιμᾶτε, πατρὸς μητέρ' 'Αλκμήνην ἐμοῦ
ξένους τε τούσδε. κἄν ἀπαλλαγῇ πόνων
καὶ νόστος ὑμῖν εὑρεθῇ ποτ' ἐκ θεῶν,
μέμνησθε τὴν σώτειραν, ὡς θάψαι χρεὼν·
κάλλιστά τοι δίκαιον· οὐ γὰρ ἐνδεὴς
ὑμῖν παρέστην, ἀλλὰ προύθανον γένους.
τάδ' ἀντὶ παίδων ἐστί μοι κειμήλια
καὶ παρθενείας, εἴ τι δὴ κατὰ χθονός·
εἴη γε μέντοι μηδέν· εἰ γὰρ ἕξομεν
κἀκεῖ μερίμνας οἱ θανούμενοι βροτῶν,
οὐκ οἶδ' ὅποι τις τρέψεται· τὸ γὰρ θανεῖν
κακῶν μέγιστον φάρμακον νομίζεται.

HERACLIDAE, 574.

THE SACRIFICE

Our sire ; and these kind hosts : and if release
Come from your griefs, and if the gods at length
Restore you home—ah, then, remember me
Your saviour, that 'twere meet you bury me,
Bury me nobly. For I failed you not,
But for my kinsfolk yielded up my life.
For hope of babes, for flower of maidenhood
This treasure is mine—if any such, indeed,
There be for us who pass beneath the sod :
Seeing none there may be ; since if there, even
      there,
Still cares await us who are set to die—
Ah ! whither shall we turn us then ? For Death
We count of griefs the cure that cannot fail.

M. VALERIVS MARTIALIS

Quid tibi nobiscum est, ludi
    scelerate magister,
inuisum pueris uirginibusque
    caput?

Nondum cristati rupere si-
    lentia galli;
murmure iam saeuo uerberi-
    busque tonas.

Tam graue percussis incudi-
    bus aera resultant,
causidicum medio cum faber
    aptat equo.

THE SCHOOLMASTER

OH, what have we to do with you,
  You usher—woe betide you?
The lads detest you, so they do,
  The lasses can't abide you.

Before the ruddy-crested cocks
  Have broke the morning silence,
Your angry growls, your thumps and knocks,
  The folk may hear a mile hence.

So rings the echoing metal with
  The anvil's clangs and clamours,
When on his steed of bronze the smith
  Some lawyer's statue hammers.

93

Mitior in magno clamor furit
    amphitheatro,
uincenti parmae cum sua
    turba fauet.

Vicini somnum non tota
    nocte rogamus ;
nam uigilare leue est, perui-
    gilare graue.

Discipulos dimitte tuos ; uis,
    garrule, quantum
accipis ut clames accipere ut
    taceas ?

                            ix. 69.

THE SCHOOLMASTER

Not half so vile the row you hear
  At shows from each spectator,
When howling crowds applaud some dear
  Victorious gladiator.

To let us sleep the livelong night
  Is more than we petition ;
Merely to wake at times were slight—
  'Tis hard sans intermission.

So let them go, the girls and boys ;
  O man of endless spouting,
D'you want as fee to hold your noise
  What now you're paid for shouting ?

ΤΥΡΤΑΙΟΣ

Τεθνάμεναι γὰρ καλὸν ἐνὶ προμάχοισι
πεσόντα
ἄνδρ' ἀγαθὸν περὶ ᾗ πατρίδι μαρ-
νάμενον.
τὴν δ' αὐτοῦ προλιπόντα πόλιν καὶ
πίονας ἀγροὺς
πτωχεύειν πάντων ἐστ' ἀνιηρότα-
τον,

πλαζόμενον σὺν μητρὶ φίλῃ καὶ πατρὶ
γέροντι
παισί τε σὺν μικροῖς κουριδίῃ τ'
ἀλόχῳ.

96

DEATH OR VICTORY

OH, Death is only Glory
  When foremost in the fight
The hero falls, a-battling
  For Fatherland and Right.
But when he quits his fatherland,
  The fields where he was born,
And turns himself to beggary,
  His lot is utter scorn.

His aged sire beside him,
  And she that gave him life,
And all his little children
  And his tender wedded wife ;

ΤΥΡΤΑΙΟΣ

ἐχθρὸς μὲν γὰρ τοῖσι μετέσσεται, οὕς
κεν ἵκηται
χρησμοσύνῃ εἴκων καὶ στυγερῇ
πενίῃ,
αἰσχύνει τε γένος, κατὰ δ᾽ ἀγλαὸν
εἶδος ἐλέγχει,
παισὶ δ᾽ ἀτιμίη καὶ κακότης ἕπεται.

εἰ δ᾽ οὕτως ἀνδρός τοι ἀλωμένου οὐ-
δεμί᾽ ὥρη
γίγνεται, οὔτ᾽ αἰδὼς οὔτ᾽ ὄπις οὔτ᾽
ἔλεος,
θυμῷ γῆς περὶ τῆσδε μαχώμεθα καὶ
περὶ παίδων
θνήσκωμεν ψυχέων μηκετὶ φειδόμενοι.

ὦ νέοι, ἀλλὰ μάχεσθε παρ᾽ ἀλλήλοισι
μένοντες

DEATH OR VICTORY

Hateful is he to all men
  That meet him by the way,
Who yields himself to poverty
  And sordid want a prey.
He brings dishonour on his race,
  Belies the form he bears,
And all contempt and vileness
  Are the portion of his heirs.

Since for the roving outcast
  No reverence is in truth,
No least respect is granted,
  No courtesy nor ruth—
Then march we forth high-hearted
  To battle for our land,
And die to guard our children,
  With our life in our right hand.

So shoulder still to shoulder
  Let every gallant fight,

μηδὲ φυγῆς αισχρᾶς ἄρχετε, μηδὲ
φόβου,
ἀλλὰ μέγαν ποιεῖσθε καὶ ἄλκιμον ἐν
φρεσὶ θυμόν,
μηδὲ φιλοψυχεῖτ' ἀνδράσι μαρνά-
μενοι.

τοὺς δὲ παλαιοτέρους, ὦν οὐκέτι γού-
νατ' ἐλαφρά,
μὴ καταλείποντες φεύγετε, τοὺς
γεραιούς·
αἰσχρὸν γὰρ δὴ τοῦτο μετὰ προμάχοισι πεσόντα
κεῖσθαι πρόσθε νέων ἀνδρὰ παλαιό-
τερον,

ἤδη λευκὸν ἔχοντα κάρη πολιόν τε
γένειον,
θυμὸν ἄποπνείοντ' ἄλκιμον ἐν κονίῃ
αἱματόεντ' αἰδοῖα φιλαῖς ἐν χεροὶν
ἔχοντα—

100

And never start a-croaking,
  And never head the flight.
Rouse up great hearts and valiant,
  Nor care a jot for life
When foeman faces foeman
  In the crash of mortal strife.

The men of ancient prowess,
  Whose limbs are stiff with years—
Oh, never fly and leave them,
  A prey to coward fears.
For shame it is to look on
  When foremost in the war
The veteran falls a-dying,
  While the lads are fleeing far.

White-haired, grey-bearded, gasping out
  His brave heart on the ground,
His bloody fingers writhing
  And clutching at the wound—

ΤΥΡΤΑΙΟΣ

αἰσχρὸν τ' ὀφθάλμοις καὶ νεμεσητὸν
ἰδεῖν—
καὶ χρόα γυμνωθέντα· νέοισι δὲ πάντ'
ἐπέοικεν
ὀφρ' ἐρατῆς ἥβης ἀγλαὸν ἀνθὸς
ἔχῃ·
ἀνδράσι μὲν θηητὸς ἰδεῖν, ἐρατὸς δὲ
γύναιξίν
ζωὸς ἐών, καλὸς δ' ἐν προμάχοισι
πεσών.

TYRTAEUS.

Oh, sight of shame to gaze on,
  Of bitter wrath and pain—
With limbs all stark and naked
  He lies upon the plain.

While glows the flower of lovely youth,
  The young its gifts may prize ;
To be admired by eyes of men,
  Lovely in women's eyes   .
While life shall last—till gloriously
  In front of fight he dies.

P. VERGILIVS MARO

At pater Aeneas, audito nomine Turni,
deserit et muros, et summas deserit arces,
praecipitatque moras omnes, opera omnia
    rumpit,
laetitia exultans, horrendumque intonat
    armis :
quantus Athos, aut quantus Eryx, aut
    ipse coruscis
cum fremit ilicibus quantus, gaudetque
    nivali
uertice se attollens pater Apenninus
    ad auras.
Iam uero et Rutuli certatim et Troes et
    omnes

THE MEETING

FATHER Aeneas, hearing Turnus' name,
Springs from the walls, springs from the
    lofty towers,
Starts every laggard into sudden haste,
Breaks up each gang, in fierce exulting
    joy.
Horribly clang his arms—as Athos huge
Or Eryx, or himself, the giant mount
Murmurous with rustling of his holm-oaks,
    crowned
With snows atop, and joying in his crown,
Old Apennine, who heaves his head to
    heaven.
Rutulians, Trojans, sons of Italy,

conuertere oculos Itali, quique alta
  tenebant
moenia, quique imos pulsabant ariete
  muros ;
armaque deposuere humeris. Stupet
  ipse Latinus,
ingentes genitos diuersis partibus
  orbis
inter se coiisse uiros, et cernere ferro.

AENEID, xii. 697.

All stayed to stare in emulous amaze ;
Who held the rampart, as who dashed the
    ram
Against its base, their weapons dropped to
    ground.
Astonied stood Latinus' self, to see
Those men of might, born half the world
    between,
Crash in the stern arbitrament of steel.

ΗΣΙΟΔΟΣ

Φράζεσθαι δ', εὖτ' ἂν γεράνου φων-
ὴν ἐπακούσῃς
ὑψόθεν ἐκ νεφέων ἐνιαύσια κεκλη-
γυίης,
ἥ τ' ἀρότοιό τε σῆμα φέρει καὶ χεί-
ματος ὥρην
δεικνύει ὀμβρηροῦ, κραδίην δ' ἔδακ'
ἀνδρὸς ἀβούτεω,
δὴ τότε χορτάζειν ἕλικας βοῦς ἔνδον
ἐόντας.
ῥηίδιον γὰρ ἔπος εἰπεῖν· 'βόε δὸς ·
καὶ ἄμαξαν.'
ῥηίδιον δ' ἀπανήνασθαι· 'πάρα δ' ἔργα
βόεσσιν.'

THE FARMER'S TEXT

MARK you the day when the clang of the
   crane's shrill voice you shall hear,
Crying aloft in the clouds, as he doth in the
   fall of the year,
Warning of earing-time, and the winter rains
   that are near:
Smiting the heart of the man who hath no oxen
   at all—
Mark it, and get you fodder for each horned ox
   in the stall.
   Easy to say, 'Come, lend me a yoke and a
      waggon, I pray';
Easy to answer, 'No; I have work for my oxen
   to-day.'

φησὶ δ᾽ ἀνὴρ φρένας ἀφνειὸς πήξασ-
· θαι ἅμαξαν,
νήπιος· οὐδὲ τό γ᾽ οἶδ᾽· ἑκατὸν δέ τε
δούρατ᾽ ἀμάξης,
τῶν πρόσθεν μελέτην ἐχέμεν οἰκήια
θέσθαι.

εὖτ᾽ ἂν δὴ πρώτιστ᾽ ἄροτος θνητοῖσι φανείη,
δὴ τότ᾽ ἐφορμηθῆναι ὁμῶς δμῶές τε
καὶ αὐτός
αὔην καὶ διερὴν ἀρόων ἀρότοιο καθ᾽
ὥρην,
πρωὶ μάλα σπεύδων, ἵνα τοι πλήθωσιν
ἄρουραι.
ἔαρι πολεῖν· θέρεος δὲ νεωμένη οὔ σ᾽
ἀπατήσει.
νειὸν δέ σπείρειν ἔτι κουφίζουσαν
ἄρουραν.
νειὸς ἀλεξιάρη, παίδων εὐκηλή-
τειρα.

THE FARMER'S TEXT

Saith he, the rich in schemes, 'Go to, I can
 build me a wain'?
Ignorant fool, whose knowledge is nought and
 his fancying vain!
Pieces there be that go to the framing a wain
 five score:
See thou choose them betimes, and keep them
 ready in store.
 Straight when the autumn comes, and the
 first of the ploughing is due,
Up and away, thyself and thy folk, while the
 season is new,
Ploughing the sandy soil as the loam, that the
 whole may be tilled,
Never an hour be lost, and so thy fields shall
 be filled.
Turn the soil in the spring, and when summer
 is come once more,
New ploughed land shall not fail, nor yield thee
 a niggardly store.

εἴχεσθαι δὲ Διὶ χθονίῳ Δημήτερί
θ᾽ ἁγνῇ,
ἐκτελέα βρίθειν Δημήτερος ἱερὸν
ἀκτήν,
ἀρχόμενος τὰ πρῶτ᾽ ἀρότου, ὅτ᾽ ἂν
ἄκρον ἐχέτλης
χειρὶ λαβὼν ὄρπηκα βοῶν ἐπὶ νῶτον
ἵκηαι
ἔνδρυον ἑλκόντων μεσάβων· ὁ δὲ
τυτθὸς ὄπισθε
δμῶος ἔχων μακέλην πόνον ὀρνίθεσσι
τιθείη
σπέρμα κατακρύπτων· εὐθημοσύνη
γὰρ ἀρίστη
θνητοῖς ἀνθρώποις κακοθημοσύνη δὲ
κακίστη.
ὧδέ κεν ἁδροσύνῃ στάχυες νεύοιεν
ἔραζε,
εἰ τέλος αὐτὸς ὄπισθεν Ὀλύμπιος
ἐσθλὸν ὀπάζοι,

New-ploughed land must be sown while the
clods are broken and light ;
Safety from harm doth it bring, and thy little
ones' quiet delight.
Pray to the Earth-lord Zeus, and the holy
Mother entreat,
So to make heavy her glory, the full-ripe ears
of the wheat.
Pray at the first of the ploughing, with hand on
the plough-tail's point,
Goading the backs of the kine, while the yoke-
thongs strain on the joint.
Armed with his hoe let the lad follow after thee,
making a toil
Hard for the fowls of the air, as he covers the
grain with the soil.
Carefulness most of all is a blessing to mortal
men,
Carelessness most of all to mortal men is a
bane.

ἐκ δ' ἀγγέων ἐλάσειας ἀράχνια· καί
σε ἔολπα
γηθήσειν βιότου αἱρεύμενον ἔνδον
ἐόντος.

WORKS AND DAYS, 448.

Thus shall the ears bow down with their
fatness nodding to earth,
So the Olympian grant that the ending match.
with the birth,
Thus from each vessel and jar thou wilt keep
the spider-web clear ;
Thus do I promise thee joy, partaking the
garnered cheer.

Q. VALERIVS CATVLLVS

Suffenus iste, Vare, quem
probe nosti,
homo est uenustus et dicax et
urbanus,
idemque longe plurimos facit
uersus.
Puto esse ego illi millia aut
decem aut plura
perscripta, nec sic ut fit in
palimpseston
relata ; chartae regiae, noui
libri,
noui umbelici, lora rubra,
membrana

THE POETASTER

FITZJENKYN—you know him, my
Hobson, I know—
Is 'good form' as they say, and
endowed with a flow
Of the best conversation—all cul-
ture!—and then,
The number of verses that run off
his pen!
I should think there are thousands
some dozen or so ;
And he don't turn them out cheap
and nasty—oh, no!
Small   quarto—the   last   shape
(which couldn't be bettered) ;

directa plumbo, et pumice
omnia aequata.
Haec cum legas tu, bellus ille
et urbanus
Suffenus unus caprimulgus aut
fossor
rursus uidetur: tantum ab-
horret ac mutat.
Hoc quid putemus esse? qui
modo scurra
aut si quid hac re tritius
uidebatur,
idem infaceto est infacetior
rure,
simul poemata attigit, neque
idem unquam
aeque est beatus ac poema
cum scribit:
tam gaudet in se, tamque se
ipse miratur.

The binding by Zaehnsdorf, in
vellum, gold-lettered ;
Handmade paper, of course, with
gilt top and rough edges—
But—Read his productions! A
yokel, a clown,
A professional trimmer of ditches
and hedges
Our elegant cultured Fitzjenkyn
is grown.
So changed, so—transmogrified!
What have we here ?
Only now 'twas a wit—though
that's hardly, I fear,
A refined enough word. And no
crude country spot
Is so crude as this very same
fellow, God wot,
Once he gets to his verses—yet
never you know him

Nimirum idem omnes fallimur
neque est quisquam
quem non in aliqua re uidere
Suffenum
possis. Suus cuique attributus
est error,
sed non uidemus manticae
quod in tergo est.

xxii

So happy as while he is scribbling
    a poem.
He's so pleased and so proud of
    himself all along ;
And :—
    MORAL.—No doubt we're all
    equally wrong,
There's no one you can't prove, in
    something or other,
A Fitzjenkyn; we've each our pet
    folly, my brother,
And we don't find the beam in our
    own eye a bother !

ΕΥΡΙΠΙΔΗΣ

Λαβὼν δ' ὑφάσμαθ' ἱρὰ θησαυρῶν
παρὰ
κατεσκίαζε, θαύματ' ἀνθρώποις ὁρᾶν.
πρῶτον μὲν ὀρόφῳ πτέρυγα περιβάλλει
πέπλων,
ἀνάθημα Δίου παῖδος οὕς Ἡρακλέης
Ἀμαζόνων σκυλεύματ' ἤνεγκεν θεῷ.
ἐνῆν δ' ὑφανταὶ γράμμασιν τοιαίδ'
ὑφαί·
Οὐρανὸς ἀθροίζων ἄστρ' ἐν αἰθέρος
κύκλῳ·
ἵππους μὲν ἤλαυν' ἐς τελευταίαν φλόγα
Ἥλιος, ἐφέλκων λαμπρὸν Ἑσπέρου
φάος.
μελάμπεπλος δὲ Νὺξ ἀσείρωτον ζυγοῖς
ὄχημ' ἔπαλλεν· ἄστρα δ' ὡμάρτει θεᾷ.

122

TAPESTRIES

FORTH of the store he drew the woven robes,
And spread them over, marvellous to view.
First, on the roof, like to a sheltering wing
He laid the tapestries, the treasure rare
Of the son of Zeus : the same that Herakles
Brought for the god, spoils of the Amazons.
There was that web, so with devices woven
As I shall tell you.   Uranus was there,
Mustering the stars in the wide arch of heaven.
There Helios urged his steeds to where their
    flame
Fades : trailing after him the glow of Eve :
And Night, mirk-shrouded, drave her swaying
    car—
No traces hold her steeds, but yokes alone—
And star on star circled the goddess round.

Πλειὰς μὲν ᾖει μεσοπόρου δι' αἰθέρος,
ὅ τε ξιφήρης Ὠρίων· ὕπερθε δὲ
Ἄρκτος στρέφουσ' οὐραῖα χρυσήρει
    πόλῳ.
κύκλος δὲ πανσέληνος ἠκόντιζ' ἄνω
μηνὸς διχήρης, Ὑάδες τε ναυτίλοις
σαφέστατον σημεῖον, ἥ τε φωσφόρος
Ἕως διώκουσ' ἄστρα. τοίχοισιν δ'
    ἔπι
ἤμπισχεν ἄλλα βαρβάρων ὑφάσματα,
εὐηρέτμους ναῦς ἀντίας Ἑλληνίσιν,
καὶ μιξόθηρας φῶτας, ἱππείας τ' ἄγ-
    ρας
ἐλάφων λεόντων τ' ἀγρίων θηράματα.

ΙΟΝ, 1141.

Through the mid-heaven a Pleiad sped her
    flight,
And sword in hand Orion hurled ; the Bear
Her quarters wheeled above in the golden sky.
On high the orbed moon darted her beams,
Full circle at the parting of the month.
There were the Hyades, that sailors know
Their surest sign ; and there the Morning rose
Herald of light, chasing the stars away.

    And on the walls more tapestries he hung,
Wrought by the cunning of the foreign folk :
Galleys, the foes of Hellas, driven with oars ;
And monstrous things, half-woman and half-
    beast ;
The mounted hunters of the stag ; the chase
Of lions fell.

M. VALERIVS MARTIALIS

EDICTUM domini deique nostri,
quo subsellia certiora fiunt,
et puros eques ordines recepit,
dum laudat modo Phasis in theatro,
Phasis purpureis rubens lacernis,
et iactat tumido superbus ore :

Tandem commodius licet sedere,
nunc est reddita dignitas equestris ;
turba non premimur nec inquinamur ;

Haec et talia dum refert supinus,
illas purpureas et arrogantes
iussit surgere Leitus lacernas.

v. 8.

THE SNOB

Lo, in the stalls our Phasis lounged to see,
And praised our lord and master's new decree
Reserving seats more strictly, so that knights
Find no mere snobs encroaching on their rights.
Phasis, resplendent in a scarlet cloak,
These swelling words with lofty accents spoke :

' At last a gentleman at ease may sit ;
Once more our knightly rank finds deference fit :
The Great Unwashed no longer jostle Us.'

E'en while at length outsprawled he mouthed it
  thus,
That flaunting scarlet Leitus espies,
And to those splendours, ' Come, turn out ! ' he
  cries.

ΑΡΙΣΤΟΦΑΝΗΣ

Ἀέναοι Νεφέλαι
ἀρθρῶμεν φανεραὶ δροσερὰν φύσιν
    εὐάγητον,
πατρὸς ἀπ' Ὠκεανοῦ βαρυαχέος
ὑψηλῶν ὀρέων κορυφὰς ἔπι
δενδροκόμους, ἵνα
τηλεφανεῖς σκοπιὰς ἀφορώμεθα,
καρπούς δ' ἀρδομέναν ἱερὰν χθόνα,
καὶ ποταμῶν ζαθέων κελαδήματα,
καὶ πόντον κελάδοντα βαρύβρομον·
ὄμμα γὰρ αἰθέρος ἀκάματον σελα-
    γεῖται
μαρμαρέαις ἐν αὐγαῖς

128

THE CLOUDS

CLOUDS ever-fleeting are we,
  And we rise into light
  In our dewy forms bright
From the arms of our father, the thunderous sea,
  From the deep-voiced Sea,
  To the towering mountain's tree-plumed crest,
  Where on far-seen summits our sight may rest;
  And we look on the holy soil
  Whose moisture ripens her fruitful store,
And the sacred streams with their wild turmoil,
  And the loud sea's roar.
For the eye of the sky never tires
As it beams with its twinkling fires.

ΑΡΙΣΤΟΦΑΝΗΣ

ἀλλ' ἀποσεισάμεναι νέφος ὄμβριον
ἀθανάτας ἰδέας, ἐπιδώμεθα
τηλεσκόπῳ ὄμματι γαῖαν.

NUBES, 275.

But come, let us shiver aside
From our forms that never shall die
The showery mists that around us abide,
And gaze over earth with a far-seeing eye.

ΕΥΡΙΠΙΔΗΣ

Μακρὰν ἂν ἐξέτεινα τοῖς δ' ἐναντία
λόγοισιν, εἰ μὴ Ζεὺς πατὴρ ἠπίστατο
οἷ' ἐξ ἐμοῦ πέπονθας οἷα τ' εἰργάσω.
σὺ δ' οὐκ ἔμελλες τἄμ' ἀτιμάσας λέχη
τερπνὸν διάξειν βίοτον ἐγγελῶν ἐμοὶ,
οὐθ' ἡ τύραννος, οὐθ' ὁ σοὶ προσθεὶς
    γάμους
Κρέων ἀνατὶ τῆσδέ μ' ἐκβαλεῖν χθονός.
πρὸς ταῦτα, καὶ λέαιναν εἰ βούλει,
    κάλει,
καὶ Σκύλλαν, ἣ Τυρσηνὸν ᾤκησεν
    πέδον,
τῆς σῆς γὰρ ὡς χρῆν καρδίας ἀνθη-
ψόμην.

MEDEA, 1351.

A WOMAN SCORNED

AT wordy length I might have met thy
    words.
But God he knoweth all that I have wrought
For thee,—and all that thou hast wrought by
    me.
My couch dishonoured, little hope for thee
To pass in scorn of me the careless days ;
Thee nor thy queen ; nor that ill match-
    maker
Creon, to cast me out nor suffer harm.
So, call me tigress, Scylla, if thou wilt,
[Scylla that dwelt upon the Tyrrhene plain]
For my gripe wrung thy heart-strings ;
    fittingly.

M. VALERIVS MARTIALIS

CUM rogo te nummos sine pignore,
    non habes inquis,
    idem si pro me spondet agellus
    habes.
Quod mihi non credis ueteri Telesine
    sodali,
    credis colliculis arboribusque meis.
Ecce reum Carus te detulit; adsit
    agellus.
    Exsilii comitem quaeris? agellus
    eat.

xii. 25.

THE FRIEND

You'd nothing, when on just my note of hand
  I asked a loan ;
You've plenty, for a mortgage on the little farm
  I own.
What, Mr. Smith! no credit for your chum of
  bygone years,
But credit for his cabbages and timber, it
  appears.
What's this? run in? oh, get that Farm to see
  you through—not me.
Need—'change of air'? Well, take that Farm
  along for company,

ΕΥΡΙΠΙΔΗΣ

Ναῦς δ' ἕως μὲν ἐντὸς ἦν
λιμένος, ἐχώρει, στομία διαπερῶσα δὲ
χάβρῳ κλύδωνι συμπεσοῦσ' ἠπείγετο.
δεινὸς γὰρ ἐλθὼν ἄνεμος ἐξαίφνης νεὼς
ὤθει πάλιν πρυμνῇσι'· οἱ δ' ἐκαρτέρουν
πρὸς κῦμα λακτίζοντες· ἐς γῆν δ' ἔμπαλιν
κλύδων παλίρρους ἦγε ναῦν. σταθεῖσα δὲ
Ἀγαμέμνονος παῖς ηὔξατ', ὦ Λητοῦς κόρη
σῶσόν με, τὴν σὴν ἱερίαν, πρὸς Ἑλλάδα
ἐκ βαρβάρου γῆς, καὶ κλοπαῖς σύγγνωθ' ἐμαῖς.
φιλεῖς δὲ καὶ σὺ σὸν κασίγνητον, θεά,
φιλεῖν δε κἄμε τοὺς ὁμαιμόνους δοκεῖ.
ναῦται δ' ἐπευφήμησαν εὐχαῖσιν κόρης

136

THE FLIGHT

NOW while within the harbour bounds, the ship
Sped steadily ; but as she passed the bar
She met a mighty billow, and was driven ;
For there a furious squall burst suddenly,
That hurled her hard astern. Howbeit, the crew
Strove stoutly, in hot struggle with the surge.
A second time back-swirling toward the shore
The wave swept. Then did Agamemnon's child
Stand up and pray : 'O Maid, of Leto born !
Save me, thy priestess, from the stranger's land,
Restore me to my Hellas, and forgive
That theft of mine. Thou, goddess, lovest thy
　　brother—
And shall not I love those that are mine own ?'
And at the damsel's prayer, the sailors raised

ΕΥΡΙΠΙΔΗΣ

παιᾶνα, γυμνὰς ἐκβαλόντες ὠλένας
κώπῃ προσαρμόσαντες ἐκ κελεύσματος.
μᾶλλον δὲ μᾶλλον πρὸς πέτρας ᾔει σκάφος·
χὠ μέν τις ἐς θάλασσαν ὡρμήθη ποσίν,
ἄλλος δὲ πλεκτὰς ἐξανῆπτεν ἀγκύλας.
κἀγὼ μὲν εὐθὺς πρὸς σὲ δεῦρ' ἀπεστάλην,
σοὶ τὰς ἐκεῖθεν σημανῶν, ἄναξ, τύχας.

IPHIGENIA IN TAURIS, 1391.

138

THE FLIGHT

A cheer for Amen, clapping hands to the oar
Bare from the shoulder, to the boatswain's pipe.
But near and nearer drove she toward the rocks.
Then one, feet foremost, leaped into the sea,
And one upon a rope made fast a noose ;
And I post-haste was hither sent to thee,
To tell thee all, O king, that there befell.

ΒΑΚΧΥΛΙΔΗΣ

τίκτει δέ τε θνατοῖσιν εἰράνα με-
γάλα
πλοῦτον καὶ μελιγλώσσων ἀοιδᾶν
ἄνθεα,
δαιδαλέων τ' ἐπὶ βωμῶν θεοῖσιν αἴ-
θεσθαι βοῶν
ξανθᾷ φλογὶ μῆρα τανυτρίχων τε
μήλων,
γυμνασίων τε νέοις αὐλῶν τε καὶ
κώμων μέλειν.
ἐν δὲ σιδαροδέτοις πόρπαξιν αἰθᾶν
ἀραχνᾶν ἱστοὶ πέλονται·

PEACE

OH, Peace is the mother of rich delight,
  For she brings us wealth, and the minstrels
    raise
  The rare sweet notes of their honeyed lays ;
And the altars brave of the gods are bright

With the yellow glow of the limbs aflare
  Of kine and of long haired goats and sheep ;
  And the lads are free to wrestle and leap,
And piping and revel are all their care.

Red spiders weave their gossamer thread
  O'er the steel-shod thongs of the shield on
    the ledge :

ΒΑΚΧΥΛΙΔΗΣ

ἔγχεά τε λογχωτὰ ξίφεά τ' ἀμφάκεα
δάμναται εὐρώς·
χαλκεᾶν δ' οὐκ ἔστι σαλπίγγων κτύπος·
οὐδὲ συλᾶται μελίφρων ὕπνος ἀπὸ βλε-
φάρων,
ἀμὸν ὃς θάλπει κέαρ.
συμποσίων δ' ἐρατῶν βρίθοντ' ἀγυιαί,
παιδικοί θ' ὕμνοι φλέγονται.

PEACE

And the rust makes spoil of the broadsword's
   edge,
And blunts the point of the keen spear-head.

The bray of the brazen trump is stilled,
   No more sweet sleep is snatched from our
   eyes
When it warms our hearts : love songs arise,
And with lovers and comrades the ways are
   filled.

Q. VALERIVS CATVLLVS

Paene insularum, Sirmio,
insularumque
ocelle, quascumque in
liquentibus stagnis
marique uasto fert uterque
Neptunus,
quam te libenter quamque
laetus inuiso,
uix mi ipse credens Thy-
niam atque Bithynos
liquisse campos et uidere
te in tuto.
O quid solutis est beatius
curis,

THE HOME-COMING

SIRMIO, the gem, the crown of isles and semi-
isles that rest

Or upon the limpid lake or rolling sea, on
Neptune's breast,

Great content and great delight are mine, to see
thee once again

Scarce assured that I have really left behind the
Thynian plain,

Left Bithynia far behind me, and in safety gaze
on thee!

Oh! the joy of troubles ended, mind from weight
of care set free,

cum mens onus reponit, ac
 peregrino
labore fessi uenimus larem
 ad nostrum
desideratoque adquiescimus
 lecto.
Hoc est quod unum est pro
 laboribus tantis.
Salue, o uenusta Sirmio
 atque ero gaude :
• gaudete uosque, o Libyae
 lacus undae :
ridete quidquid est domi
 cachinnorum.

xxxi.

When all travel-worn and weary back to our
  own hearth we come,
On the pillow that we yearned for rest our head
  once more at home—
Compensation sole, sufficient, for the trouble we
  have borne.
Welcome, lovely isle of Sirmio! Greet your
  lord on his return!
Waves of Libya gladly greet me, greet me waters
  of the mere,
All the smiles and happy laughter of the home-
  stead give me cheer.

ΣΟΦΟΚΛΗΣ

νῦν δ' οὐδέν εἰμι χωρὶς, ἀλλὰ πολλάκις
ἔβλεψα ταύτῃ τὴν γυναικείαν φύσιν,
ὡς οὐδέν ἐσμεν· αἳ νέαι μὲν ἐν πατρὸς
ἥδιστον οἶμαι ζῶμεν ἀνθρώπων βίον·
τερπνῶς γὰρ ἀεὶ πάντας ἀνοία τρέφει.
ὅταν δ' ἐς ἥβην ἐξικώμεθ' ἔμφρονες,
ὠθούμεθ' ἔξω καὶ διεμπολώμεθα
θεῶν πατρῴων τῶν τε φυσάντων ἄπο,
αἱ μὲν ξένους πρὸς ἄνδρας αἱ δὲ βαρ-
        βάρους,
αἱ δ' εἰς ἀήθη δώμαθ', αἱ δ' ἐπίρροθα.
καὶ ταῦτ', ἐπειδὰν ἡμέρα ζεύξῃ μία,
χρεὼν ἐπαινεῖν καὶ δοκεῖν καλῶς ἔχειν.

TEREUS (fr. 517).

WOMAN'S LOT

BUT now, myself alone, I am nought at all.
Nay, oft in thought thus have I brooded o'er
Our woman's nature, and our woman's lot,
That we are nought. Oh, we young girls at home
Live lives the sweetest mortals may, no doubt,
Since pleasure still is fed by lack of thought.
But when we grow to womanhood and wit,
We are thrust out from the nest, trafficked away
Far from our parents and our fathers' gods,
This to a friend, this to some outlander,
This to a home with strange new ways, and this
To one contemptible.   And when the bond
For a single day has yoked us, we—why, straight
We must applaud, and count it very good.

M. VALERIVS MARTIALIS

AMISSUM non flet cum sola est
  Gellia patrem :
si quis adest iussae prosiliunt
  lacrimae.

Non dolet hic, quisquis laudari,
  Gellia, quaerit :
ille dolet uere qui sine teste
  dolet.

i. 35.

THE MOURNER

GELLIA, sitting all alone,
Weeps not for her father gone ;
But if friends to see her go,
Quickly summoned tears will flow.

Gellia, 'tis but grief to feign
When you weep applause to gain ;
His the grief that's real and deep,
Who when none is by will weep.

ΕΥΡΙΠΙΔΗΣ

Ἅρματα μὲν τάδε λαμπρὰ τεθρίππων
ἥλιος ἤδη λάμπει κατὰ γῆν
ἄστρα δὲ φεύγει πῦρ τόδ' ἀπ' αἰθέρος
ἐς νύχθ' ἱεράν,
παρνησιάδες δ' ἄβατοι κορυφαὶ
καταλαμπόμεναι τὴν ἡμερίαν
ἀψῖδα βροτοῖσι δέχονται.
σμύρνης δ' ἀνύδρου καπνὸς ἐς ὀρόφους
Φοίβου πέτεται.

θάσσει δὲ γυνὴ τρίποδα ζάθεον
Δελφίς, ἀείδουσ' Ἕλλησι βοάς
ἃς ἂν Ἀπόλλων κελαδήσῃ.
ἀλλ' ὦ Φοίβου Δελφοὶ θέραπες,

THE MINISTER OF PHOEBUS

EVEN now the bright sun with his burning rays
Is kindling his four-horsed car to a blaze
Over the earth ; and the stars take flight
From the flame of the sky to the sacred night.
The pathless peaks of Parnassus aglow
   Are catching the gleam of his arc for men ;
See the smoke of the myrrh unwatered go
   Floating up to the roof of the sun-god's fane.

On the holy tripod the dame is throned,
And the Hellenes list to her cry intoned—
The Delphic priestess, who takes the word
From the mystic chant of Apollo her lord.
You Delphian servants of Phoebus, away

ΕΥΡΙΠΙΔΗΣ

τὰς Κασταλίας ἀργυροειδεῖς
βαίνετε δίνας, καθαραῖς δὲ δρόσοις
ἀφυδρανάμενοι στείχετε ναούς·
στόμα τ᾽ εὔφημον φρουρεῖν ἀγαθὸν,
φήμας τ᾽ ἀγαθὰς τοῖς ἐθέλουσιν
μαντεύεσθαι
γλώσσης ἰδίας ἀποφαίνειν.

ἡμεῖς δὲ πόνους οὓς ἐκ παιδὸς
μοχθοῦμεν ἀεί, πτόρθοισι δάφνης
στέφεσίν θ᾽ ἱεροῖς ἐσόδους Φοίβου
καθαρὰς θήσομεν ὑγραῖς τε πέδον
ρανίσιν νοτερόν, πτηνῶν τ᾽ ἀγέλας,
αἳ βλάπτουσιν
σεμν᾽ ἀναθήματα, τόξοισιν ἐμοῖς
φυγάδας θήσομεν· ὡς γὰρ ἀμήτωρ
ἀπάτωρ τε γεγὼς τοὺς θρέψαντας
Φοίβου ναοὺς θεραπεύω.

ΙΟΝ, 82.

Where the silvery eddies of Castaly play ;
Then haste to the temple, made pure with her
    spray.   .
Take heed that your words be the words that
    are meet,
And the speech that your lips speak still be
    discreet,
To them that are seeking the counsels divine.

And straight will I turn to the task that is mine,
And ever hath been from my childhood's days.
With sacred wreaths and with laurel sprays
The precinct of Phoebus I 'll purify,
    And sprinkle the lawn with a moistening dew,
    And with my arrows the feathered crew
That foul His treasure I 'll make to fly.
Since orphaned of parents I was born,
Since never a mother I knew, forlorn,
Nor father, mine is the ministry
Of the Temple of Phoebus that fostered me.

M. VALERIVS MARTIALIS

NON coenat sine apro noster, Tite,
·   Caecilianus ;
bellum   conuiuam   Caecilianus
habet.

vii. 59.

THE BOON COMPANION

FITZ-DOBBIN never cares to dine
Without a boar at table ; why ?
Because Fitz-Dobbin cannot shine
But in congenial company.

INDEX

INDEX

INDEX

Printed by T. and A. CONSTABLE, Printers to Her Majesty
at the Edinburgh University Press